# ZACHARY'S DINNERTIME

by
Lara Levinson

Illustrated by
Cornelius Van Wright

Star Bright Books
Massachusetts

Published in the United States of America by Star Bright Books, Inc.

The name Star Bright Books and the Star Bright Books logo are registered trademarks of Star Bright Books, Inc. Please visit www.starbrightbooks.com. For bulk orders, email: orders@starbightbooks.com.

Hardback ISBN-13: 978-1-59572-329-1
Paperback ISBN-13: 978-1-59572-330-7

Star Bright Books / MA / 00109110
Printed in China (WKT) 10 9 8 7 6 5 4 3 2 1

Library of Congress Cataloging-in-Publication Data

Levinson, Lara.
    Zachary's dinnertime / by Lara Levinson ; illustrations by Cornelius Van Wright.
        p. cm.
    Summary: Although Zachary's parents ask him to help, he does not like helping his family at dinnertime to do such things as set the table, peel potatoes, or wash the dishes, but when he visits the homes of friends for a week, he has a change of heart.
    ISBN 978-1-59572-329-1 (hardcover) -- ISBN 978-1-59572-330-7 (pbk.)
    [1. Dinners and dining--Fiction. 2. Family life--Fiction. 3. Food habits--Fiction.] I. Van Wright, Cornelius, ill. II. Title.
    PZ7.L57925Zac 2012
    [E]--dc23
                        2011032387

*For Amelia* —L.L.

*To Ying-Hwa* — C.VW.

Every night, Zachary ate dinner with his father, his mother, and his little sister, Emily.

Every night, Zachary's parents asked him to help set the table. Forks on the left. Knives and spoons on the right. Salad bowls on the side. Glasses at the top.

Every night, Zachary's parents asked him to help prepare dinner. Peel the potatoes. Chop the vegetables. Toss the salad.

Every night, Zachary's parents asked him to help clean up after dinner. Clear the table. Wash the dishes. Dry the dishes.

And every night, Zachary wished that he could be a guest in someone else's home. Where no one would ask him to help set the table. Where no one would ask him to help prepare dinner. And where no one would ask him to help clean up after dinner.

So, for one week, Zachary didn't come home for dinner. He went to his friends' homes instead.

Monday night he went to Yukiko's home. Yukiko's family is Japanese-American and served a traditional Japanese meal of fish and rice.

But Zachary was a guest. So he wasn't asked to help set the table with chopsticks and bowls. He wasn't asked to help broil the fish or to steam the rice. He wasn't asked to put the decorative trays back in the cupboard.

And Zachary was sorry he couldn't help.

Tuesday night Zachary went to Elisa's home. Elisa's family is Mexican-American and served a traditional Mexican meal of rice, beans and enchiladas.

But Zachary was a guest. So he wasn't asked to help set the table with salsa bowls. He wasn't asked to help stuff the enchiladas. He wasn't asked to help dry the tortilla holder after it was washed.

And Zachary was sorry he couldn't help.

Wednesday night, Zachary
went to Guy's home. Guy's family
is Israeli-American and served a
traditional Israeli meal of hummus,
falafel, pita and salad.

But Zachary was a guest. So he wasn't asked to help set the table with the good silverware. He wasn't asked to help roll the falafel balls. He wasn't asked to clear the table after dinner.

And Zachary was sorry he couldn't help.

Thursday night, Zachary went to Edward's home. Edward's family is African-American and served a traditional African-American meal of chicken, fish, yams and plantains.

But Zachary was a guest. So he wasn't asked
to prepare the spice rub. He wasn't asked to help
cut the plantains. He wasn't asked to put away the
serving platters.

And Zachary was sorry he couldn't help.

Friday night Zachary went to Samir's home. Samir's family is Indian-American and served a traditional Indian meal of chicken curry and nan bread.

But Zachary was a guest. So he wasn't asked to help set out the samosas and chutney. He wasn't asked to help mix the curry spices. He wasn't asked to help put the silver platter back in its place.

And Zachary was sorry he couldn't help.

Saturday night, Zachary returned home for dinner and invited all of his friends.

His parents were serving chicken
with mashed potatoes and vegetables.
And Zachary no longer wanted to
be a guest.

Before his parents even asked, he
helped set the table. He helped steam the
vegetables and mash the potatoes.

He helped wash every
dirty dish and put each one
back in the cupboard.

And his parents said, "Thank you!"